Praise for the Series

"*T*hese are the stories I've been waiting to read since childhood — classic tales, vividly retold, and beautifully illustrated in ways that stimulate the imagination. The questions posed are important ones to young minds — how things happen and why, as well as the consequences of personal choices. They are what I pondered as a child experiencing my own twists and turns in life. And those were the thoughts that very much influenced my becoming a writer. As these stories show, there are no simple answers, but with imagination you can go to many places and find many possibilities. These are magical stories for everyone."

— Amy Tan
Award winning and best-selling writer
Author of "The Joy Luck Club"
Creative Consultant to the PBS television series "Sagwa"

"*As a child, these tales nourished my imagination and ability to love and to hate. They introduced me to fantasy lands full of characters with courage, integrity and goodness. They made me understand that tragedies are not necessarily sad, because tender hearts usually achieve happiness and satisfaction through sorrow. In a word, they have made me what I am today, a writer, whose livelihood depends on compassion and fascination.*

As modern renditions and artful adaptations of these ancient tales, this series has brought out the most touching elements and core spirit, drama and beauty of the old stories, yet at the same time given them a new life and charm catered to young readers today."

— Geling Yan
Award winning writer
Author of "The Banquet Bug"

"*As my daughters are getting older, I have been wanting them to know the best stories from the Chinese culture, but have found it hard to locate a version with the right kind of story-telling suitable to their ages and 'American' taste, that could draw and hold their attention, and strike a chord in their hearts.*

I am happy to have been presented this series. Beautiful stories beautifully retold, in a refreshing way and with age appropriate gradings, this edition is the finest I've ever seen, definitely something I would like my children to read and grow up on."

— Joan Chen
Award winning actress/director
Leading role, "The Last Emperor"

The Butterfly Lovers

梁山伯与祝英台

Teri Tao

Golden Peach Publishing

Text and illustrations copyright © 2008 by Golden Peach Publishing LLC

Published by Golden Peach Publishing LLC
1223 Wilshire Blvd., #1510
Santa Monica, CA 90403, USA
www.goldenpeachbooks.com
editorial@goldenpeachbooks.com

ISBN: 978-1-930655-14-0
Printed in China
First printing, May 2008

Editing, translation and notes by Nina Tao
English copy-editing by Rashid Williams-Garcia
Illustrations by Ning Hu
Book design by Yang Hui

Once upon a time in Zhejiang, China, there was a river called "Jade Water River". Half way encircled by the river was a village called "Zhu's Village". In the village there was a big, well-off family of generations of scholars. The youngest generation consisted of nine children, eight boys and one girl.

The only girl, named Zhu Ying-tai, was also nicknamed "Little Nine" as she was the youngest of all. Mr. Zhu had sent all his children to the private school in the village, except Ying-tai, because in those days girls were not allowed to go to school, but rather, expected to stay home to learn sewing and embroidery and other household skills. Ying-tai's heart was filled with envy seeing her brothers going to school every day.

从前，在中国的浙江，有一条玉水河，河边有个祝家庄。祝家庄里有个大户人家，祖祖辈辈都是读书人。祝老爷夫妇生有九个孩子，八个男孩子，最小的是女孩子，叫祝英台，小名叫九妹。祝老爷把八个男孩子都送到了私塾，只有英台不能上学。那时候，女孩子是不能读书的，只能呆在家里，学做衣服，学绣花。英台看着哥哥们每天上学，非常羡慕。

From time to time, Ying-tai would secretly follow her eight brothers to school and listen to the teacher from outside the window.

Once, the teacher asked a question no one in the class could answer. Ying-tai could not help uttering from outside, "I know!"

The teacher was so surprised to find it was a little girl. He let her in and asked her a few more questions, but she had perfect answers to all. The teacher shook his head. "What a shame! What a shame you are a girl!" he sighed.

英台常常悄悄跟在八个哥哥身后到学校去，趴在教室的窗台外偷偷听老师讲课。有一次，老师在上课的时候提问，大家都答不出来，窗外祝英台忍不住伸进头来说："老师，我能回答！"老师惊异地看到是个小小的女孩子，就叫她进来。一连问她好多问题，英台全都对答如流。老师连连摇头："可惜啊，可惜！可惜你是个女孩子！"

One day, Ying-tai's parents went in their study and found a little boy they didn't know reading there, his face buried in a big, thick book.

"Who are you?" Mr. Zhu asked.

The boy turned around, his eyes sparkling from trying to hold back a laugh. Mr. and Mrs. Zhu both thought that he looked familiar, but still could not make out who he was. Then the boy burst out laughing, whisked off his hat and let out his long hair. It was not a boy, but Ying-tai in her brother's clothes! Amused and also a little annoyed, her parents didn't know what to say.

　　一天，祝老爷和夫人刚进书房的门，就看到一个不认识的男孩子坐在书桌前，捧着厚厚的一大本书，聚精会神地阅读着。祝老爷问："你是哪家的孩子啊？"这个男孩子忍着笑回过头来。祝老爷和夫人觉得眼熟，又想不起这到底是谁，一时都愣住了。男孩子哈哈大笑起来，突然摘掉了帽子，露出长长的头发，原来是穿着哥哥衣服的英台！祝老爷夫妇哭笑不得。

Ying-tai jumped into her parents' arms and announced, "Dad! Mom! I want to go to school!"

Mr. Zhu stroked his daughter's long hair and sighed, "How can a girl go to school? No school would admit a girl student!"

"But I can dress as a boy!" Ying-tai exclaimed. "Even I didn't recognize you in those clothes. I guess others will not be able to tell," Mrs. Zhu smiled and commented. With her mother on her side, Ying-tai would not let her father leave the room until he agreed to send her to school in a boy's disguise. Mr. Zhu finally gave in.

From then on, Ying-tai started going to school with her brothers.

英台扑到他们怀里：“爸！妈！我要读书！”祝老爷怜爱地摸着女儿的头发，说：“女孩子怎么能读书呢？没有学堂收女学生啊！”英台说：“我可以女扮男装啊！”祝夫人笑道：“连我这当妈的都没看出来，看来是瞒得过别人的。”有妈妈撑腰，英台一定要爸爸也同意允许她装扮成男孩子去读书，否则不让爸爸出门。爸爸只好同意了。从此，英台和哥哥们一起上学了。

Not long after Ying-tai went to school did she become the top student of the whole class. She graduated in less than a year, and would have to go to Hang Zhou Academy for further study. Hang Zhou was very far from home, a long boat ride and a lot of walking. Ying-tai managed to persuade her worried parents that she would be fine.

She left with a huge bag of books and in boy's clothes, of course. Right before she got on the boat to leave, Ying-tai hugged her parents and told them that she had left them with a surprise gift at home in her dad's study. Back home, Mr. and Mrs. Zhu found a self-portrait of their daughter on the wall of the study, looking back at them with a big smile on her face.

不久，英台的成绩就排到了最前面，不到一年就毕业了。要想继续求学，只能去杭州城的杭州书院了。杭州离家很远，水路要撑船，旱路要步行，爸爸妈妈很不放心。英台好不容易才说服了他们，背了一大口袋书离开了家。临上船前，英台抱住爸爸妈妈，调皮地说："我给你们留了一个好东西，就在爸爸书房里！"祝老爷夫妇回到家里，书房墙上赫然挂着一张祝英台的自画像。画上的英台活灵活现，笑眯眯地看着爸爸妈妈。

Ying-tai's boat had followed the water of the Jade Water River and arrived at a dock by Straw Bridge. From this point on, Ying-tai would have to walk, and the road to Hang Zhou Academy on top of Ten Thousand Pine Mountain was eighteen miles long.

Dragging her disintegrating book bag, Ying-tai made her way ahead slowly. Just then, a tall boy rushed over to her.

"Take a break at the Straw Bridge Pavilion over there! I'll help you with the bag!" he said, and handed Ying-tai a handkerchief while taking the heavy book bag from her shoulder.

祝英台的小船在玉水河顺流而下，到草桥码头停了下来。从草桥到万松岭上的杭州书院，还要走十八里山路。英台拖着快要散包的大书口袋，一步一步地向前挪着。正在这时，迎面快步走来一个高个男孩子。他在英台面前站下，说："到那边草桥亭里休息一下吧，我来帮你！"说着，他递给英台一条汗巾，又从英台手里拿下沉重的书口袋。

Ying-tai just realized that she was sweating and panting.

"I am also going to school at Hang Zhou Academy. We could walk there together!" the boy said. Ying-tai smiled. She felt happy and relieved to have this nice, warm, big brother-like boy for company.

'Wow! It is so beautiful out here,' she just noticed. Small bridges over clear streams, willows billowing in the wind, birds chirping. The tiny pavilion called Straw Bridge Pavilion actually looked quite elegant and cozy. How come she hadn't seen all this before?

"What's your name?" she asked the tall boy. "Liang Shan-bo," he told her.

英台这才注意到，自己已经是满头大汗了。"我也是去杭州书院读书的，咱们可以一路同行啊！"看着这个憨厚、热情、像大哥哥一样的男孩子，英台心里一阵高兴。哇，这里这么漂亮！小桥流水，杨花柳絮，鸟语花香，那个叫草桥亭的小亭子更是清雅秀美。刚才怎么都没看到啊！"你叫什么？"她问男孩子。"梁山伯。"男孩子回答。

Shan-bo put Ying-tai's big book bag on his shoulder and led her to the pavilion. Helping her tidy up the loose bag so that the books would not fall out, he said, "Wow, you have the same books as me!"

Ying-tai felt surprised too that her brothers never liked or understood the books she loved, yet this Liang Shan-bo liked to read exactly the same books as she did. How different was he than regular boys!

"If only I had a brother like you!" she sighed.

梁山伯扛起英台的大书口袋，拉着英台一起坐到了草桥亭里。他一边帮助她整理已经散了的包裹，一边说："怎么你带的书和我带的都一样啊！"英台也觉得很奇怪，她爱看的书，都是哥哥们不喜欢也看不懂的，怎么这个梁山伯也这么爱看书，和一般的男孩子这么不一样？想着，她叹了口气说："要是我有一个你这样的哥哥就好了！"

"Why don't we become sworn brothers?" Shan-bo suggested immediately. "We could take care of each other on the road and in school too," he added. Ying-tai jumped to her feet. "Good idea!" she exclaimed.

"But I've heard that you have to burn some incense and pray to make it work!" Shan-bo said.

"That's not a problem. We could just find some willow branches to use as substitute!" replied Ying-tai.

Shan-bo marveled at how smart his new friend was. Ying-tai found some willow branches on the ground near the pavilion. Using these as incense, the two "boys" swore to be brothers.

梁山伯马上说：“那咱们结拜成兄弟好了！一路上和学堂里，也好互相有个照顾！”英台跳起来说：“好哇！”梁山伯说：“可是听说古人结拜，都是要烧香的啊！”祝英台说：“那有什么难的，咱们到亭子外找几根柳枝来就好啦！”“对对，还是贤弟聪明，只要心诚，柳枝也行！”英台到亭子外面找到几根柳枝，两人请柳树为证，拜为兄弟。

When it was time to get back on the road, Shan-bo found a big long stick to use as a shoulder pole to carry Ying-tai's book bag and his own, one on each end. The two of them talked about poetry and other fine writings as they walked. Ying-tai was so happy and she found herself talking a lot. Before long, they were on the other side of the mountain.

"Hey Shan-bo, let me take the bags for a while!" Ying-tai offered.

"No need. You are a year younger than me, and you are so little! You can't be as strong as I am," Shan-bo replied. 'How would he know that I am actually a girl?' Ying-tai thought to herself.

　　山伯找到一根木棍，把自己和英台的大书口袋一头一个，全挑在了肩上，两人一起上路了。他们一路谈书、谈诗，英台兴高采烈，滔滔不绝。不知不觉，已经翻过了一座山，又过了一道弯。"山伯兄，让我挑一会儿吧！"英台说。"不用，你比我小一岁，还这么瘦小，身体一定不如我！"山伯回答。英台想，他哪知道，我是女孩子啊！

Soon the two of them reached the Ten Thousand Pine Mountain, and Hang Zhou Academy came into sight. Ying-tai handed back the handkerchief Shan-bo had handed to her earlier.

"Why don't you keep it?" said Shan-bo. "You don't seem to have yours with you." Ying-tai thanked him. "We are brothers now, you don't have to thank me for a little thing like that," Shan-bo smiled. "By the way Ying-tai, you are really amazing. You are so little yet you know so much! I've never met anyone I enjoy talking with so much, really," Shan-bo continued.

Ying-tai felt a little shy. She lowered her head to fiddle with Shan-bo's handkerchief in her hand, yet her heart was filled with joy.

两人上了万松岭，杭州书院就在眼前了。英台要把汗巾还给山伯，山伯说："你没带汗巾来，留着用吧。"英台说："那谢谢了！"山伯说："都是兄弟了，不必这么客气。英台弟，别看你身材不高，可是学问真是很大，我还从来没遇到过一个能这样谈古论今的同学呢！我说的是真的。"英台低下头，手里摆弄着山伯的汗巾，心里甜甜的。

At school, Shan-bo and Ying-tai spent a lot of time together as classmates. They went to class, played music, wrote poetry, and practiced martial arts together. At each exam and test, either Ying-tai scored first place, Shan-bo second, or the other way around. Soon the two became known as the best students in the whole school.

Before they knew it, three years had passed and Shan-bo had now grown from a lanky boy into a handsome young man. Ying-tai had also become, well, a good looking "guy" in other people's eyes, although nobody else knew about the changes she was going through inside....

山伯和英台开始了朝夕相处的同学生活。他们在一起听课讨论，一起弹琴赋诗，一起打拳练剑。每次考试，或山伯第一、英台第二，或英台第一、山伯第二，两个人很快成了书院中最优秀的学生。一晃，三年过去了。山伯从一个清瘦的小男生长成了一个英俊的小伙子。英台呢，在别人看起来，也是一个英俊的"小伙子"。但是英台心里，却悄悄地发生了变化……

From time to time, Ying-tai had the urge to tell Shan-bo that she was actually a girl. Often she dreamed about herself walking side by side with Shan-bo, in a long dress and with flowers in her hair. She was afraid though once truth was told, she would not be able to stay in school, which meant she would not be able to spend more time with Shan-bo. Every minute she had with him she savored with great gratitude.

Earlier that year, both Shan-bo and Ying-tai had taken the Imperial Examination, but before they received their scores, Ying-tai got a letter from her father, asking her to quit school and go home right away for a family emergency.

英台真想告诉山伯自己是个姑娘，她常常梦见自己身穿长裙，头插鲜花，在山伯面前走过。但她又怕一旦大家都知道了，她就不能再与山伯同窗共读了。和山伯在一起的每一分钟，她都觉得是幸福的。正是那一年，山伯和英台一起报考了状元。还没开榜，英台突然收到一封父亲的来信，说家里有急事，不让她留在书院念书了，催她快快回家。

Ying-tai went to see Shan-bo with the bad news. She could not stop her tears from running down her cheeks when she saw his concerned eyes.

"We boys don't cry, remember? I'll see you off to the Straw Bridge Pavilion," Shan-bo consoled her.

It was the same eighteen miles they walked from the pavilion to the school three years ago. Tears in her eyes, Ying-tai swallowed what she was going to say a few times. Shan-bo was also feeling so sad that he could not speak. The two of them went down the hill quietly. 'If I don't tell Shan-bo the truth now, there might not be another chance', Ying-tai thought to herself. But how could she begin?

英台见到山伯，眼泪不禁扑簌簌掉下来。山伯安慰英台说："咱们是大小伙子，别哭啊。我会送你到草桥的！"书院到草桥的十八里路，是三年前他们上学来的时候一起走过的。英台眼含泪花，欲言又止，山伯也难过得说不出话来，两个人默默地下了山。英台想，现在要是不对山伯说出心里话，以后恐怕就没机会说了。可是该怎么说出口呢？

As the two of them reached the outskirts of Hang Zhou, they saw a farmer walking by, carrying something heavy with a shoulder pole. Right behind him they saw his young wife wearing bright green and red, grinning happily as she hopped along after him.

Ying-tai said to Shan-bo: "Look at that farmer. He's carrying everything so his wife would not need to carry anything. Just like what you are doing!"

"He is doing this for his wife, but I'm doing this for my little brother. It isn't the same," Shan-bo said dryly.

Ying-tai sighed.

两人出了杭州城，迎面一个农夫挑着沉重的担子走过来，后面跟着一个穿红带绿、美滋滋的小媳妇。英台停下来，对山伯说："你看这位农夫，把担子都挑在自己肩上，不肯劳累他的媳妇，就和你一样啊！"山伯笑了，说："他是为他媳妇，我是为我兄弟，我们不一样的。"英台叹了一口气。

Then the two walked by a lotus pond and saw a pair of mandarin ducks floating side by side among the green lotus leaves.

Ying-tai thought of using this scene to drop a hint to Shan-bo, so she said, "Shan-bo, look at the duck couple swimming together. They are enjoying each other's company just like us!"

Shan-bo laughed and said, "No, my silly little brother, mandarin ducks are metaphors for couples. How could we be like them?"

Ying-tai sighed.

两人路过一片莲花池。莲花朵朵，荷叶青青，两只鸳鸯并肩在水中游着。英台想，我何不用再这情景暗示一下山伯？就对山伯说："山伯兄啊，你看这鸳鸯成双成对，相亲相爱，就和我们一样！"山伯笑了，说："傻兄弟，鸳鸯戏水，是用来比喻夫妻情深的，咱们俩怎么能像鸳鸯一样呢？"英台叹了一口气。

When they came to a single log bridge, Ying-tai held her steps at the sight of the rapidly flowing water underneath. Shan-bo immediately rushed over and offered to help. He grabbed Ying-tai's hand and carefully walked her over to the other end of the bridge.

"Shan-bo, look at us, don't we look just like Cowherd Boy and Weaver Girl on the Magpie Bridge?" Ying-tai said softly.

"Ying-tai, you are joking again. How could we brothers be like that famous couple?" Shan-bo laughed.

Ying-tai sighed, more deeply this time.

两人走过一座独木小桥。英台看了一眼桥下，河水很急，禁不住停下了脚步。山伯看到了，立刻过来说："小心！我来扶你！"山伯拉住英台的手，一步一步走上了桥。英台低声道："山伯兄，你看咱们这样，像不像牛郎织女上了鹊桥啊？"山伯笑了："英台，你又在开玩笑，咱们兄弟俩怎么能像牛郎织女呢？"英台叹了一口气。

"Stop sighing, Ying-tai. Listen to the cowherd singing over on the other hill. What a nice song!" Shan-bo stopped walking and told Ying-tai.

"It doesn't matter how well the cowherd sings. The cows would just never understand! I've been like that cowherd all this time, singing to a dumb cow in vain!" Ying-tai complained.

Shan-bo was taken aback a little. A minute later he asked, "You mean I am like the cow?" Ying-tai turned around to hide her tears. "Only dumber!" she sighed. Shan-bo rubbed his head and didn't know what to say.

山伯停下脚步，说："英台，别叹气了，你听那边山坡上，牧童唱的山歌多好听！" 英台说："牧童唱得再好听，牛也不会懂啊。我就像那牧童，一路上都在对牛弹琴啊！"山伯愣了一下："英台，你是说我像那牛吗？"英台转过身去，含着眼泪说："你比牛还笨啊！"山伯摸了摸脑袋，不知说什么好。

Seeing that Ying-tai was in tears, Shan-bo said, "Don't be sad, Ying-tai. We'll arrive at Straw Bridge Dock in a minute and you'll soon be on the boat. Why don't you just tell me what you have on your mind?"

Ying-tai thought for a moment, then raised her head up and started hesitantly: "Shan-bo, do you have someone in your heart that you want to marry?"

"Me? How would I have that! You know me!" Shan-bo laughed. "If you don't, then... then...I...." Somehow Ying-tai just could not bring herself to say it.

"Then what? Tell me!" Shan-bo urged.

看见英台眼泪汪汪，山伯赶紧劝慰道："英台，不要难过了，马上就要到草桥码头，你就要上船了，有什么话咱们赶紧说吧！"英台想了又想，终于抬起头来，开口说："梁兄，不知你是不是有意中人？"山伯说："我哪有什么意中人，你还不知道我！""要是没有，那，我……""你怎么样？说啊！"

"I...I have a twin sister named Little Nine. She looks just like me and she has a heart like mine. If you wish, you could come to our house to propose to her," Ying-tai finally said, with quite some difficulty.

Shan-bo smiled. "If she looks like you and has a heart like yours, I'd be more than happy to! After we graduate next month, I'll come to your house to propose." Shan-bo paused for a moment, then added: "Only my family is poor and won't be a good match for yours."

"My sister is different. She does not care about money. My father is a scholar and would not mind either," Ying-tai assured him.

"我……我有一个双胞胎妹妹，叫九妹。她和我一样容貌，一样心肠，山伯兄如果有意，可以到我家来提亲。"山伯笑了："假如九妹真像你一样容貌，一样心肠，那实在是求之不得！还有一个月就毕业了，然后我就到你家去求婚！只怕山伯家贫，高攀不上哩。"英台说："九妹自幼与众不同，视身外之物为鸿毛。家父饱读诗书，也不是嫌贫爱富之人。"

As Shan-bo and Ying-tai came to the end of the eighteen-mile walk, they had to say goodbye to each other at the Straw Bridge Dock. Ying-tai took out a handkerchief and handed it to Shan-bo. Shan-bo found two embroidered butterflies on it, and their colors were amazing. "A pair of dancing butterflies! Wow! Where did you find such a beautiful handkerchief?" Shan-bo asked.

"You gave it to me three years ago when we first met, remember?" Ying-tai answered.

"But who did the embroidery?" asked Shan-bo. Ying-tai smiled. She did not say anything, but just jumped onto the boat. Her boat was soon too far to see, but Shan-bo still stood there wondering.

两人走了十八里，在草桥码头恋恋不舍地分手了。英台拿出一条汗巾递给山伯。汗巾上绣着两个互相追逐起舞的蝴蝶，色彩斑斓。山伯忍不住赞叹道："彩蝶双飞！哪儿来的这么漂亮的手巾？""你忘了，这是三年前，第一次见面的时候你给我的。""可这是谁绣的呢？"英台笑了一下，没有回答，一跃身上了船。船开出很远，山伯还拿着汗巾呆呆地站在岸上。

Ying-tai got home and asked her parents what the emergency was. They smiled and said, "It's actually nothing to worry about, but something to celebrate! Governor Ma's son has proposed to marry you! He fell for you when he visited us with his father and saw your portrait. We have already accepted the proposal, so they'll send in betrothal gifts this month and you'll get engaged!"

To Ying-tai, what her parents just told her was like thunder striking on top of her head. She almost sat on the ground. Mr. and Mrs. Zhu rushed over to hold her and asked, "What is the matter, Little Nine?"

"Dad, Mom! I already have someone in my heart, and his name is Liang Shan-bo!"

英台回到家里，见过父母，忙问有什么急事。父母笑道："不是急事，是喜事！本郡太守马老爷父子到咱家作客，看到了你的画像，马少爷一下子看中了你，我们已经答应了！这个月就要送彩礼来订婚了！"父母的话，如五雷轰顶，英台差点儿站不住了。父母忙过来扶住她，连连催问："你这是怎么了？"英台泣不成声："爸啊，妈啊，女儿已经有心上人了！他叫梁山伯！"

"Marriage should be arranged by parents. How could you make choices yourself! This is totally out of line!" Mr. Zhu struck the table and said angrily.

"My daughter, the Ma family is well-off and would be a good match to ours, plus Governor Ma is so powerful we can't really say no to them," Mrs. Zhu added.

Ying-tai wiped her tears and said firmly, "Their wealth means nothing to me compared to Shan-bo's talents; matching of two families means so much less than what Shan-bo and I feel for each other. I would rather die than marry anyone else!"

祝老爷一拍桌子："婚姻大事，应当由父母说了算，你怎么能自己去找，这成何体统！"祝夫人也对英台说："女儿啊，马太守家财万贯，和咱家也算门当户对，况且马太守权大势大，咱也得罪不起啊。"英台擦干眼泪，坚定地说："家财万贯比不上我山伯兄才高八斗，门当户对比不上我和山伯兄情投意合。我宁死也不会嫁给别人！"

From that day on, Ying-tai would stand on her balcony, stare at the Jade Water River, and wait for Shan-bo to come.

One day at dusk, a small boat appeared in the distance, with a tall young man standing on the front, his long scholar robe billowing in the wind. Ying-tai immediately recognized that it was Shan-bo! She jumped with joy, and raised her arms high up to wave at him.

At this moment, a big boat decorated with lanterns and huge ribbons appeared from behind Shan-bo's boat. Ying-tai's heart sank. Was it Governor Ma's boat sending over the betrothal gifts? And sure enough, she saw her parents rushing out to meet them, in their best clothes.

从此，英台每天站在楼台之上，望着蜿蜒流过的玉水河，等待着山伯。这天傍晚，她看到河面上漂来一叶扁舟，从小舟上迎风站立的翩翩身影，她一下子认出来，梁兄到了！英台高兴得跳起来，举起手使劲挥舞着。突然，一艘大船从后面驶来，大船上张灯结彩，好不气派。英台心中一沉，难道是马老爷家的送彩礼来了？果然，祝老爷夫妇已穿戴齐整，出门迎候了。

Just when Shan-bo's small boat was about to dock by Ying-tai's house, the big boat behind forced its way ahead. With a loud cracking sound, it knocked Shan-bo's boat over and Shan-bo fell into the water. The Zhus were really surprised and angry to see Governor Ma was being such a big bully. They sent their servants to rescue the young man from the water.

Now the big boat was already docked in front of them. Governor Ma and his son got off the boat and were walking towards them with their heads up, looking very important. With his fingers pointing to Shan-bo, the son yelled, "Who the hell are you? How dare you block my way?" Shan-bo replied, "I am Scholar Liang Shan-bo. I'm here to propose to Little Nine of the Zhu family."

山伯的小船刚要在英台家门前靠岸，后面跟过来的大船横冲直撞地开了过来，轰的一声，把小船撞翻了。祝老爷夫妇见马太守这样霸道，非常吃惊和气愤，赶紧派人把小船上落水的人救起来，大船已经开到眼前。马太守带着儿子威风凛凛地下了船，指着刚刚被救起的梁山伯问："你是什么人？怎么敢挡我的路？" 山伯站起来，"我叫梁山伯，是来向祝家九妹求婚的！"

"Little Nine is marrying ME! How DARE you make trouble with the governor's family! Take him!" the governor's son ordered his guards, who circled Shan-bo to beat him up.

Mr. Zhu rushed over to try to stop them, while Governor Ma bellowed: "Mr. Zhu, how many families are you going to marry your only daughter to?"

"I did not know that my daughter already had someone, so I agreed to your proposal by mistake. We are not engaged yet, so let's call it off," Mr. Zhu stood tall and said firmly.

"祝家九妹就要嫁给我了，你居然在这里和太守家作对，给我抓起来，打！"马少爷一声令下，家丁们一拥而上，对山伯拳打脚踢。祝老爷忙上前阻拦。马太守高喝道："祝老爷，你一个女儿许配几家？"祝老爷挺直了腰板，说："我原不知小女已有了心上人，所以贸然答应了太守的请求。现在两家尚未订婚，这门亲事，就算了吧。"

"Call it OFF?" Governor Ma raised his voice even higher. "Are you KIDDING me? Come, take this crazy old man and that Liang Shan-bo guy away and put them in jail!"

"Hold it!" a girl's voice came from upstairs. Everyone raised their heads to see a most beautiful and elegant young lady standing on the balcony above.

Afraid that Governor Ma would do something to harm his daughter, Mr. Zhu called, "Ying-tai! Go back to your room! Go!"

"Ying-tai? Ying-tai?" Shan-bo was too stunned for words.

马太守暴跳如雷道："算了？拿我们马家开玩笑吗？来人，把姓祝的老头儿和这个梁山伯抓起来，押入大牢去！"突然，楼上传来一声："住手！"大家都抬起头来。只见楼台之上，一个面如桃花、端庄优雅的姑娘临风而立。祝老爷唯恐太守加害女儿，高叫道："英台，快回去！""英台？！英台？！"梁山伯惊呆了。

'So Ying-tai is Little Nine herself? Little Nine is the Zhu Ying-tai who has been my closest friend and dear little brother for the past three years in school? Ying-tai is a girl?' Shan-bo wondered.

Shan-bo was playing back scenes from the day he was seeing Ying-tai off on the eighteen-mile walk. Outside the city Ying-tai compared the two of them to a farmer couple; by the lotus pond she compared them to a pair of mandarin ducks; on the single log bridge she compared them to Cowherd Boy and Weaver Girl. Then Ying-tai gave him back his handkerchief in which she had embroidered a pair of butterflies.... Shan-bo could not help kicking himself for having been such a "dumb cow" all this time!

　　英台就是九妹？九妹就是和我同窗三载、心心相印的祝英台？祝英台是女孩子？梁山伯眼前，浮现出十八里相送的一幕幕场景。杭州城外，英台把两人比作形影相随的农家夫妇；莲花池畔，英台把两人比作相亲相爱的鸳鸯；独木桥上，英台把两人比作鹊桥相会的牛郎织女；英台在他的汗巾上，绣上了双飞的彩蝶，寄托了无限的情意……山伯捶胸顿足，自己真是一只笨牛啊！

Governor Ma's son was also surprised, surprised to see that Ying-tai was actually even prettier than the picture of her that he had seen. He whispered something in Governor Ma's ears.

"Well, Zhu Ying-tai, if you agree to marry my son, I'll let your father and this poor student go. If not, you'll never see either of them again!" Governor Ma cleared his throat and threatened her.

Mr. Zhu stared at Governor Ma and shouted angrily, "You are despicable!"

"Ying-tai, don't! Marrying into the Ma family would be like joining a wolf pack!" Shan-bo cried.

马少爷也惊呆了。这祝英台，怎么比画上的还漂亮！他立刻趴马太守的耳朵上嘀咕了几句话。马太守说："好，祝英台，你要是同意嫁给我儿子，我就放开你爸爸和这个穷小子！要是不同意呢，你以后就别想再见到他们了！"祝老爷怒视着马太守："你无耻！"梁山伯叫道："英台，不要答应他们！进了马府，就是进了狼窝啊！"

Tears rolled down Ying-tai's cheeks. She stepped forward, and spelled out these words to Governor Ma between her teeth, "I'll marry your son if you let them go!"

Ma's son was so happy to hear this that he shouted, "Quick! Let them go! Ying-tai, I'll take you home tomorrow!"

His father gave him a stern look. "How is tomorrow possible? Haven't we already chosen a good day for the wedding? We'll come back in a month to take her!" he told him.

"Then I'll stay in the Zhu's Village a little longer so I could see my beauty everyday!" the son replied.

祝英台热泪滚滚。她向前迈了一步，一字一句地对马太守说："你们放开他们，我就嫁给你的儿子！"马少爷喜得抓耳挠腮，连声说："快，快放开他们！英台啊，我明天就把你娶回家！"马太守瞪了他一眼："明天怎么行？不是算好了良辰吉日了吗？一个月后，我们再过来迎亲！"马少爷马上说："那我就要在祝家庄小住几天，也好朝夕见到我的美人！"

Mr. Zhu prepared a boat for Shan-bo and asked him to leave as quickly as possible.

The Moon was covered up by dark clouds, and the river was flowing rapidly, making a weeping sound. Shan-bo's boat took off and disappeared slowly into the darkness. Ying-tai stood by her window looking. Her heart went with the boat. For hours she didn't move. Now it was deep in the night and all was quiet.

Suddenly, Ying-tai heard a familiar voice calling her name. Could it be Shan-bo coming back for her? Sure enough, it was Shan-bo right under her balcony!

祝老爷赶紧为梁山伯备了一只小船，说，"孩子啊，快离开这里吧！"乌云遮月，河水呜咽。山伯的小船离开了岸边，渐渐隐没在夜幕里。英台身在楼台上，心却被小船牵走了。不知过了多久，英台还是一动没动，呆呆地站在窗前。夜深人静，万籁俱寂。突然，英台听到一声熟悉的呼唤，难道山伯回来了？果然，山伯正在楼下！

Ying-tai was so surprised and happy! She let down a rope from the window to let Shan-bo climb up to her room.

Their hands joined together and their tearful eyes met.... At the break of dawn they felt that they still had a lot more to say to each other. Shan-bo took out the handkerchief with Ying-tai's butterflies and said, "Wait for me! The exam results will be out soon. If I turned out to be the Number One Scholar, I'd be able to punish the evil Governor Ma!"

"I'll never part with you no matter what happens. If we could not live together, we could choose to die together. I'll be with you, in life and in death!" Ying-tai re-assured him.

英台又惊又喜，急忙从窗口垂下一条绳子。山伯沿着绳子爬到了楼台之上。双手紧握，泪眼相对。东方渐渐露出了鱼肚白，两个人还有很多心里话没说完。山伯拿出彩蝶双飞的手巾，说："等着我，马上就要开榜了，我要是中了状元，就能惩治马太守那恶霸了！"英台说："你放心，生不同床死同穴，我生生死死都要和你在一起！"

Ying-tai waited and waited for Shan-bo to return but he did not. Today was her scheduled wedding day with the governor's son. The bridal sedan was already in front of her house, with a loud band playing noisy wedding tunes.

In her red dress and red head cover, Ying-tai was a crying mess in her parents' arms. The governor's son got impatient and yelled from downstairs, "Ying-tai! Come down here already! Your Shan-bo is dead! Just forget about him and come with me!"

Ying-tai could not believe her ears! She passed out at this horrible news. "Where is Shan-bo buried?" was the first thing she asked after she awoke.

英台望穿秋水，不见山伯回转。今天就是马府迎亲的日子了，吹吹打打的花轿已经停在楼台之下。英台穿上红色嫁衣，头戴盖头，和爸爸妈妈哭作一团。马家少爷急了，在下面大喊道："英台，快下来吧！你那梁兄早就命赴黄泉了，赶紧死了心跟我走吧！"英台一听，晕了过去。她醒过来的第一句话就是："梁兄埋在哪里？"

What had happened was that Shan-bo had been wounded by Governor Ma's people earlier and his condition worsened day by day as he missed Ying-tai terribly after he got back to school. Finally he could not hold up any longer. He called Ying-tai's name a few times before he passed, tightly holding the butterfly handkerchief in his hands....

Now Ying-tai had stopped crying. She changed into a white dress, put a white ribbon in her hair, and then walked downstairs to tell her parents: "I am going to be married off today. Please pack up and leave this place yourselves." Then she turned to the governor's son: "Take me to Shan-bo's grave site first, or else I would never marry you!"

　　原来山伯回去后，伤势越来越重，加上忧思悲愤，卧床不起。一天，他连连呼叫了几声"英台"，便离开了人世，手中还紧紧攥着英台绣的彩蝶双飞的汗巾……英台不再哭泣，换上一身雪白的衣裙，头上扎一条雪白的发带，走下楼来，对父母说："女儿要出嫁了。你们赶紧收拾一下东西，远走高飞吧。"又对马家少爷说："先带我去看梁兄的墓，不然我绝不嫁给你！"

The wedding crowd took a turn on the way to the groom's house to make a stop at Shan-bo's grave. Ying-tai slowly walked out from the bridal sedan, towards Shan-bo's tomb.

All of a sudden, she called out Shan-bo's name and dashed to his tombstone. At this moment, a big storm came, and lightning and thunder struck across the sky. "Shan-bo! Shan-bo! Here I come!" As Ying-tai cried, Shan-bo's grave split open with a deafening crack. Ying-tai trippingly made her way in, her long black hair floating, her white dress billowing as she jumped.

The grave slowly closed, while the heavy rain and wind all came to a sudden stop, and a rainbow appeared across the sky.

迎亲队伍绕道而行,来到了梁山伯墓。英台缓步下轿,向山伯坟前走去。突然,她叫着山伯的名字,哭着向墓碑上猛撞过去。一时间,风雨交加,雷电大作。"山伯!山伯!我来了!"随着英台的呼唤,山伯的坟墓轰的一声爆裂了。只见英台白裙飘飘,长发飞扬,翩然跃入了坟中。坟墓慢慢合拢了。风停了,雨息了,云开雾散,一道彩虹横上了天空。

In front of the wedding crowd from both the Ma's and Zhu's families, there appeared two colorful, gigantic butterflies from the grave, dancing and fluttering close by each other.

Just then, a horseback messenger rushed over and exclaimed, "Congratulations, Mr. Zhu! Liang Shan-bo and Zhu Ying-tai have tied in the Imperial Examination and both have won the Number One Scholar!"

Mr. Zhu was not paying any attention and seemed to have heard nothing. He was staring at the two butterflies that Ying-tai and Shan-bo had transformed into, chasing each other up and down, flying around freely, higher and higher up into the sky, until they could no longer be seen....

在马、祝两家迎亲嫁女的队伍惊愕的注视下，坟墓中飞出两只色彩斑斓的蝴蝶，你追我逐，双双起舞。这时，一个身穿官服的人骑着骏马飞跑过来，高喊着："大喜啊，祝老爷！梁山伯和祝英台高榜得中状元，并列第一名！"祝老爷好像什么也没听见，出神地看着山伯和英台化成的两只蝴蝶，他们自由自在地追逐飞舞着，越飞越高，越飞越远……

Notes on Chinese Culture

1. Private School
(私塾, sī shú, P5)

Children (boys only, that is) were sent to private schools in the old days in China at age 7 or 8 to learn reading and writing. Only private schools were available, so only rich people could afford to send their children to school. Usually the schools would keep them for several years, to about the equivalent of middle school level nowadays. Higher level education was available in some big cities where there were institutes and academies, such as the Hang Zhou Academy in this story.

2. The Imperial Examinations
(考状元, kǎo zhuàng yuán, P19, P46)

They were held once a year in old China to select talented young people to work as government officials in different levels. The person who did the best in the exam would be called "the Number One Scholar" (状元) and guaranteed a high-ranking job, prestigious social status and wealth throughout his life.

As the story tells us, women's rights were very limited and girls were not allowed to go to school at all. The "best" future for a girl coming of age would be to marry well.

3. Sworn Brothers
(结拜兄弟, jié bài xiōng dì, P14)

It was a tradition in ancient China for men who were close with one another to become sworn brothers. It was often between/among young scholars or warriors. The usual ceremony would involve burning incense to pray to Heaven to bless them, drinking wine and kow-towing to Heaven and Earth together. Once sworn, the "brothers" would help and support each other for the rest of their lives, and would even give their lives for one another.

Notes on the Series

The *Enchanted Tales of China* series, as part of the *Golden Peach Chinese Culture Readers* program, collects and retells the most treasured, timeless Chinese tales that have captured hearts and imaginations for over a thousand years.

● **Bilingual Text**
Each old story is retold in modern English for general Western readers interested in Asian cultures. In addition, the English text is supplemented by text in Chinese on the bottom of page for readers who wish to learn more of the language, or as a helpful tool for Chinese teachers or parents.

● **Leveled Format**
The series is loosely leveled for different age groups, based on their various abilities in understanding the culture, rather than their language levels. To give readers ample room for flexibilities, the levels are not distinctly marked with numbers, but only color coded for easy recognitions: the orange level targets mostly teenage readers, and the green level is more for younger children.

● **Cultural Notes**
Notes on Chinese culture will enhance readers' understanding of the stories, as well as of their historical and social backgrounds. For older readers the notes are more elaborate and detailed, while for younger audience they come in a simple format under a section entitled "Did you know…?"

● **Color Illustrations**
Full color, vibrant illustrations highlight some important scenes.